A Note to Parents

Welcome to REAL KIDS READERS, a series of phonics-based books for children who are beginning to read. In the classroom, educators use phonics to teach children how to sound out unfamiliar words, providing a firm foundation for reading skills. At home, you can use REAL KIDS READERS to reinforce and build on that foundation, because the books follow the same basic phonic guidelines that children learn in school.

Of course the best way to help your child become a good reader is to make the experience fun—and REAL KIDS READERS do that, too. With their realistic story lines and lively characters, the books engage children's imaginations. With their clean design and sparkling photographs, they provide picture clues that help new readers decipher the text. The combination is sure to entertain young children and make them truly want to read.

REAL KIDS READERS have been developed at three distinct levels to make it easy for children to read at their own pace.

- LEVEL 1 is for children who are just beginning to read.
- LEVEL 2 is for children who can read with help.
- LEVEL 3 is for children who can read on their own.

A controlled vocabulary provides the framework at each level. Repetition, rhyme, and humor help increase word skills. Because children can understand the words and follow the stories, they quickly develop confidence. They go back to each book again and again, increasing their proficiency and sense of accomplishment, until they're ready to move on to the next level. The result is a rich and rewarding experience that will help them develop a lifelong love of reading.

For Julianna, with thanks
—M. L.

Special thanks to Lands' End, Dodgeville, WI, and to Hanna
Andersson, Portland, OR, for providing clothing, and to
Ashley McBride, International, NYC, for providing bedsheets.

Produced by DWAI / Seventeenth Street Productions, Inc.
Reading Specialist: Virginia Grant Clammer

Copyright © 1998 by The Millbrook Press, Inc. All rights reserved. Published by
The Millbrook Press, Inc. Printed in the United States of America.

Library of Congress Cataloging-in-Publication Data
Leonard, Marcia.
    Spots / Marcia Leonard ; photographs by Dorothy Handelman.
        p.   cm. — (Real kids readers. Level 1)
    Summary: A girl describes her spotted clothes, rug, lamp, and mug, but her twin sister
prefers stripes.
    ISBN 0-7613-2016-4 (lib. bdg.). — ISBN 0-7613-2041-5 (pbk.)
    [1. Pattern perception—Fiction. 2. Twins—Fiction. 3. Stories in rhyme.] I. Handelman,
Dorothy, ill. II. Title. III. Series.
PZ8.3.L54925Sp   1998
[E]—dc21   98-13970
                                                                                            CIP
                                                                                            AC

pbk: 10 9 8 7 6 5 4 3 2 1
lib: 10 9 8 7 6 5 4 3 2 1

Spots

By Marcia Leonard
Photographs by Dorothy Handelman

M

The Millbrook Press
Brookfield, Connecticut

I like spots.
I like them lots.

5

I like spots that are big.
I like spots that are small.

I like spots that are blots.
But that is not all.

I have a lamp with spots.

I have a rug with spots.

13

I sip my milk
from a mug with spots.

15

I like spots on a dog.
I like spots on a ball.

I like spots on a bug.
But that is not all.

I have a hat with spots.

21

I have a dress with spots.

23

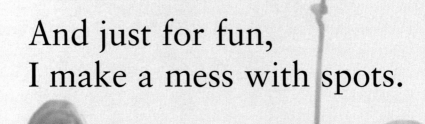

And just for fun,
I make a mess with spots.

I like to put
all my spots in one spot.

Oh, yes! I like spots.

My twin sister does not!

Reading with Your Child

1. Try to read with your child at least twenty minutes each day, as part of your regular routine.
2. Keep your child's books in one convenient, cozy reading spot.
3. Read and familiarize yourself with the Phonic Guidelines below.
4. Ask your child to read *Spots* out loud. If he or she has difficulty with a word:
   - Help him or her decode the word phonetically. (Say, "Try to sound it out.")
   - Encourage him or her to use picture clues. (Say, "What does the picture show?")
   - Ask him or her to use context clues. (Say, "What would make sense?")
5. If your child still doesn't "get" the word, tell him or her what it is. Don't wait for frustration to build.
6. Praise your beginning reader. With your enthusiasm and encouragement, your child will go from one success to the next.

Phonic Guidelines

Use the following guidelines to help your child read the words in *Spots*.

Short Vowels
When two consonants surround a vowel, the sound of the vowel is usually short. This means you pronounce *a* as in apple, *e* as in egg, *i* as in igloo, *o* as in octopus, and *u* as in umbrella. Short-vowel words in this story include: *big, bug, but, dog, fun, hat, lots, mug, not, rug, sip, yes.*

Short-Vowel Words with Beginning Consonant Blends
When two different consonants begin a word, they usually blend to make a combined sound. Words in this story with beginning consonant blends include: *skip, stop, trip.*

Short-Vowel Words with Ending Consonant Blends
When two different consonants end a word, they usually blend to make a combined sound. Words in this story with ending consonant blends include: *just, lamp, milk.*

R-Controlled Vowels
When a vowel is followed by the letter *r*, its sound is changed by the *r*. A word in this story with an *r*-controlled vowel is: *for.*

Double Consonants
When two identical consonants appear side by side, one of them is silent. Double-consonant words in this story include: *all, ball, small.*

Sight Words
Sight words are those words that a reader must learn to recognize immediately—by sight—instead of by sounding them out. They occur with high frequency in easy texts. Sight words not included in the above categories are: *a, and, are, does, from, have, I, in, is, like, make, my, oh, on, one, put, sister, that, them, to, with.*

I have read these Real Kids Readers:

Level 1

○ Big Ben
○ Dan and Dan
○ Get the Ball, Slim
○ Hop, Skip, Run
○ I Like Mess

○ My Pal Al
○ The New Kid
○ The Tin Can Man
○ Spots

Level 2

○ The Best Pet Yet
○ The Good Bad Day
○ Lost and Found
○ The Lunch Bunch
○ The Rainy Day
    Grump

○ Shoes, Shoes, Shoes
○ That Cat!
○ That's Hard,
    That's Easy
○ Too-Tall Paul,
    Too-Small Paul

Level 3

○ Lemonade for Sale
○ Loose-Tooth Luke
○ My Pen Pal, Pat
○ On with the Show!

○ That Is *Not* My Hat!
○ You're in Big Trouble,
    Brad!

REAL KIDS READERS™
Spots

Big spots and little spots, spots of all colors—this girl absolutely *loves* spots!

"Real Kids Readers are a welcome resource for helping children become skilled readers. These appealing books engage the young reader with realistic story lines and lively characters; most important, they provide needed opportunities for practicing and reinforcing essential phonic skills and sight vocabulary taught in school."

Alvin Granowsky, Ed.D.
(Dr. Granowsky has served as the Reading Consultant to the National PTA and as Director of Reading for the public schools of Greensboro, NC, and Dallas, TX.)

Level 1: Ages 4 to 6 Preschool to Grade 1

Level 2: Ages 5 to 7 Kindergarten to Grade 2

Level 3: Ages 6 to 8 Grade 1 to Grade 3

THE MILLBROOK PRESS

$3.99 U.S./Higher in Canada

ISBN 0-7613-2041-5

90000 >

E A N

9 780761 320418

R E A L
K I D S
R E A D E R S

LEVEL
1
Pre-K to Grade 1

Green Light Readers
For the reader who's ready to GO!

LEVEL

1

The Big, Big Wall

Reginald Howard
Illustrated by **Ariane Dewey and Jose Aruego**

This Green Light Reader belongs to:

I read it by myself on:

_____